THE
SANTA FE TRAIL

THE
SANTA FE TRAIL

David Lavender

Holiday House / New York

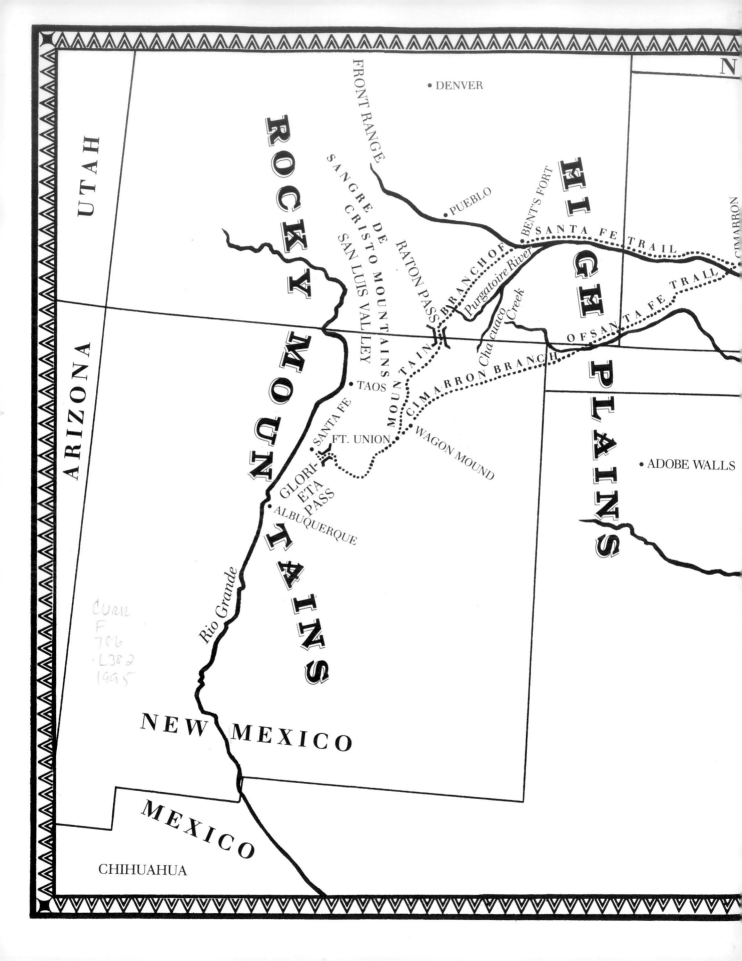

During the summer of 1821, William Becknell, a pioneer farmer of Franklin, Missouri, got the notion that Mexican rebels were on the point of winning their country's long battle for independence from Spain. How he had picked up the rumors across so many miles we do not know. Perhaps Franklin's little newspaper carried a speculative story about the course of the war. Or he may have heard the gossip at the town's landing dock, where keelboats plying the Missouri River tied up while delivering merchandise from St. Louis.

The tale certainly wasn't much to build a castle on. But that was what William Becknell did. Like many of his neighbors, he was deeply in debt. Farm produce could hardly be sold in Missouri in 1821. Jobs were scarce. Becknell's creditors were suing him. If he lost everything he had, what would become of him, his wife, and their three small children?

Mexico . . . the word shone with sudden brightness. If Mexico did indeed become independent, the new government might repeal the old Spanish laws that forbade trade with foreigners. In that case, the first group to bring desirable dry goods and hardware to the northern province of New Mexico might turn a handsome profit.

Becknell decided to put such a party together. He knew it might face severe problems. He had read the book Lieutenant Zebulon Pike had written about his exploratory trip up the Arkansas Valley and over the Front Range of the Rocky Mountains into land belonging to Spain in 1806–7. Because of this trespass, Spanish troops had arrested Pike and the American soldiers with him. For a while they were imprisoned in Santa Fe, the capital city of New Mexico. But punishing an American officer might have created more trouble with the United States than Spain wanted. So Pike and his men had been let go.

Lieutenant Zebulon Pike was the first U.S. government official to see Santa Fe. He began his adventure by following the Arkansas River to its headwater in the Rocky Mountains. Photographer, W. H. Brown, Center for Southwest Studies, University of New Mexico.

What interested Missouri frontiersmen about Pike's book was not the story of the soldier's adventures. Rather, it was the lieutenant's remark about the high prices New Mexicans were willing to pay for ordinary merchandise shipped north from far-off Mexico City. Since Franklin was a lot closer to Santa Fe than Mexico City was, transportation costs on American goods would be low and profits high. Or so the first men to follow Pike thought.

They were wrong. They, too, had been arrested by Spanish troops. Horses, goods, and furs were taken from some of them. Others were imprisoned for long terms.

William Becknell had talked to some of those men when they returned empty-handed to Franklin. Nevertheless, he decided to run the risk. The revolution might have succeeded by the time he reached New Mexico. Besides, he was used to taking chances. He had captured wild horses and had traded with Indians on the wide prairies west of the Missouri River. He felt he could take care of himself in most situations.

Because the trip was dangerous, he could persuade only five men to go with him. Loading several bales of goods onto the backs of their pack mules, they started west on September 1, 1821. For several weeks they journeyed a little south of west, finally reaching the Arkansas River in what is now the central part of Kansas.

The river valley was broad and sandy. Here and there they saw cottonwood trees close to the river. Scattered thickets of wild plums grew on sand dunes farther away from the river's crooked course. Soon they encountered weird-looking yucca, its tall stems rising out of clusters of

A wagon train carrying merchandise to New Mexico fords the Arkansas River.

long, sharp-pointed leaves. There was prickly pear cactus, too, and many rattlesnakes. The grass was very short and curly and looked too dry to make good food, but big buffalo grazed on it with relish.

Late in October the six Americans reached a small tributary river that flowed north out of the tawny hills bordering the south side of the Arkansas Valley. Long ago the little stream had been named Purgatoire (Purgatory) by French trappers. Americans, who had difficulty pronouncing French words, called it Picket Wire.

A note on Zebulon Pike's map stated that the Purgatoire marked the start of a trail that led to Santa Fe. Pike had not investigated the stream, however, but had marched his soldiers on up the Arkansas Valley to the Rockies. So when Becknell's people turned up the Purgatoire, they had no idea what lay ahead.

After several miles, the barren hills bordering the stream turned into high cliffs. Unable to continue through the narrowing canyon, the riders turned back to a branch known today as Chacuaco Creek. This brought them to a forbidding line of rocky slopes and sheer cliffs. As far as they could see, the only way to proceed was to build a risky trail up a crevice that seamed the face of the cliffs. For two days they rolled boulders out of the way of the horses. Even so, one of the animals fell from the narrow path and, in Becknell's words, "was bruised to death."

In time they reached a high, stark, cold, and dreary plain. To their right loomed the heavily forested peaks of the Sangre de Cristo Mountains, southernmost spur of the Rockies. Fresh snow powdered the summits. While angling southwest, looking for a way through the barrier, the Americans encountered outriders from a force of more than four hundred Mexican cavalrymen commanded by Don Pedro Ignacio Gallego. A whole army to contend with!

Neither the Americans nor Captain Gallego could speak the other's language. But smiles and friendly gestures were enough. The Americans were welcome. The revolution had succeeded. Mexico was an independent country. The troops were not looking for trespassers from the United States but were pursuing Apache raiders.

Vastly relieved, the Americans followed a rough road around the southern tip of the Sangre de Cristo Mountains. On November 16 they reached Santa Fe. They had been in the saddle for seventy-seven days. They estimated they were about a thousand miles from Franklin.

The community they entered was very different from their hometown. Small "ranchos" sprawled along both sides of a creek grandly named Rio San Francisco—the San Francisco River. Each ranch had a garden plot irrigated by water brought through *acequias* (canals) from the "river." Each had a shedlike barn and a corral of upright stakes where a donkey, a horse, a milk cow, some chickens, a few sheep and pigs were kept.

The single-story, flat-roofed houses were built of adobe bricks. The bricks were made by pouring wet clay into wooden molds. The molds were then placed where the clay could be baked hard by the sun. Many homeowners protected the brick walls of their houses from rain by covering them with a whitewash called yeso.

Very few of the small windows had glass. In its place were thin sheets of a partly transparent mineral called mica. If a room had a fireplace, and most did, it was built in a corner. Cooking was done in the fireplace or in an outdoor oven built of clay. People slept on mattresses spread out on the floor at night. By day the mattresses were rolled up against the walls and used as seats.

Most of the townspeople were poor. The men wore buckskin trousers. The women wore short skirts (cloth was expensive) and covered their heads with shawls. They wove their own blankets, brought in their own firewood on the backs of their donkeys, butchered their own animals for food. They were generous and hospitable, and had a deep love for their harsh, beautiful land.

The streets were full of potholes and littered with trash. The longest was San Francisco Street. It ran parallel to the creek of the same name. At its east end was a big church topped by two tall, ornate towers. The building was called La Parroquia (parish church or church). The towers were the first thing travelers saw as they approached Santa Fe.

The center of the town was an open square, or plaza. It was dusty in dry weather, muddy in wet. Visiting Indians and travelers camped there. On the plaza's north side was the Palace of the Governors. Becknell must have thought it a strange palace. It was long and low, and built of adobe.

A curious sight to the Americans was a Mexican wood seller, carrying firewood from door to door on his donkeys.

The tallest building in Santa Fe was La Parroquia, a church. Visible beyond it in the picture is an American flag flying above a fort built by the Americans immediately after the conquest of the Southwest.

On reaching Santa Fe, the capital of New Mexico, a caravan leader reports to the Mexican customs officer in front of the Palace of the Governors. Notice how scattered the buildings are and how barren the plaza in front of the palace is. *Governor's Palace, Santa Fe, 1840* by Tom Lovell. Courtesy of Abell-Hanger Foundation and the Permian Basin Petroleum Museum, Midland, Texas.

Its front side was shaded by a wooden awning, or portico, whose outside edge rested on a row of wooden posts. In back was a huge walled enclosure into which the town's horses could be driven in case of an Indian raid. Inside the palace were the offices of the provincial government. One housed the customs. There the Americans paid duties (taxes) on the merchandise they were importing from the United States.

The arrival of the six Americans in November 1821 provided the residents of Santa Fe with a totally new experience. They fell with hungry joy on the offerings displayed in a store Becknell rented. Many of the buyers paid for their purchases with silver coins called pesos, each worth one dollar in Missouri. The New Mexicans also wanted to trade furs, blankets, mules, and even piñon nuts for American goods.

Soon Becknell realized there was a shortage of pesos in New Mexico. He also learned that two other parties were on their way to Santa Fe. More would come when news of Mexico's independence reached the frontier. So he decided to hurry back to Franklin and acquire a fresh stock of merchandise before competition reduced prices, and before the town's supply of money was gone.

He started back on December 13 with a single companion. They put leather bags of pesos and furs on pack mules and took extra riding horses with them. They followed a new and easier route, described to them by Mexican buffalo hunters called *ciboleros* who ventured far out onto the plains to hunt the shaggy creatures. The way slanted northeast from the eastern foothills of the Sangre de Cristo Mountains. It crossed miles of High Plains until it reached

Prairie dogs (actually ground squirrels) lived in "towns" of burrows that often stretched for miles across the High Plains.

the mostly dry Cimarron River. The two Americans followed the Cimarron Valley from water hole to water hole. On reaching the point where the Cimarron turned sharply southeast, they left it and took a northerly course to the Arkansas River.

They were lucky. During their journey they met no blizzards and no Indians. Their only discomforts were cold rains, high winds, and lack of firewood for cooking some of their meals. They reached Franklin on January 29, 1822. The trip had taken forty-eight days as compared to the seventy-seven days they had spent on the westbound trip.

Excited by Becknell's accomplishment, two other trading parties started west. The first consisted of thirty-one men led by two rugged pioneers, Benjamin Cooper and

Joel Walker. They left in April and ran into trouble in the Arkansas Valley. Indians delayed them by stealing some of their animals. Perhaps the suffering was worthwhile, however. Prices had stayed high in Santa Fe. For example, a small handheld looking glass (mirror) that sold for a dime in Franklin brought a dollar in New Mexico.

Blizzards in the Arkansas Valley almost destroyed the second party. The men, about fifty of them, started too late in the fall and were forced to build shelters on an island where cottonwood trees provided logs. So many of their animals froze to death that they were unable to move their cargo when spring came. So they hid their bales in deep

An ox cart in front of a Pueblo Indian village. Until Americans arrived, there was not one wagon in all New Mexico.

holes, called caches, that they dug into the ground on the north side of the river. Walking and riding the few saddle horses that survived the storm, they found a way through the mountains to the little town of Don San Fernando de Taos, a few miles from the big Indian pueblo of Taos. The settlements lay sixty miles north of Santa Fe. The Americans obtained more pack stock in Taos and recovered their cached goods. Some of the party decided to live in Taos, which soon became a gathering place for trappers who hunted beaver in the central Rockies.

American traders often took part of their merchandise to Taos, a Mexican town north of Santa Fe. The Indian pueblo of Taos stood just outside the town. The round adobe object in the foreground of the picture is an oven for baking bread.

William Becknell left Franklin late in May 1822 between the two parties just described. Again he was innovative and pioneered a new way of travel in the Far West. After paying part of his debts, he bought a wagon for $150 and loaded it with as many goods as he could afford. Twenty other poor men pooled their small resources and bought two more wagons. They loaded the vehicles with bolts of calico and cotton cloth, glassware, shoes, nails, knives, and other kinds of hardware.

These were the first wagons to travel on the plains of the American West. The other two parties had used mules to transport merchandise, just as Indian traders on the frontier had been doing for years. But Becknell's ride back across the plains had convinced him that wagons could make the trip. They would be better than mules. They would not have to be unpacked every night at the campgrounds and repacked every morning. There would be less damage to fragile items. And wagons could be used as small forts in case of Indian attack.

In spite of the wagons, there was lots of trouble on Becknell's second trip. One night when the party was in camp near the Cimarron River, stampeding buffalo scattered most of their horses and mules. A few of the men who rode off in search of the strayed animals were captured by Comanche Indians, but were later ransomed by an American Indian trader. Becknell and the other members of the group did not know this. They waited for six days, searching as well as they could. Then, as they began to run out of food, they went on.

In Santa Fe, William Becknell sold for $700 the wagon

that had cost him $150. The rest of the goods were sold at similar markups. When word of the success reached Franklin, it made a profound impression. Clearly the Santa Fe trade, carried across hundreds of miles of wild country in wagons, was going to become an important part of the economy of frontier Missouri.

Franklin, however, did not share in the prosperity. A flood destroyed much of the village. At about the same time paddle-wheel steamboats began churning up the Missouri River past Franklin to the point where the river valley turned north. There the boats unloaded their cargoes at a collection of huts called Wayne City. Small wagons then carried the boxes, barrels, bales, and sacks up the steep hill behind Wayne City to the new town of Independence, Missouri. It was a hundred miles closer to Santa Fe than Franklin was.

A caravan catches its first glimpse of Santa Fe.

Independence, Missouri, was an important departure point for west-bound caravans for more than twenty years.

Businessmen in Independence built big warehouses where merchandise destined for Santa Fe could be stored until called for. By 1830 the warehouses were surrounded by blacksmith shops, harness shops, wagon shops, and grocery stores. Outside the town were pastures where hundreds of mules and oxen could graze. Quickly the town became a great trading center.

There is always room for improvement, however. A dozen miles farther up the river, developers built an easier road leading out of the Missouri River. At the end of this short road, they built the town of Westport. By the middle of the 1840s, Westport had passed Independence as a favorite starting place for westbound caravans.

The men who owned merchandise and wagons headed for Santa Fe were called proprietors. Two or three proprietors might form a partnership to outfit a single wagon. Or a single proprietor might fill several wagons. Soon Mexicans were joining in the trade. By the time Westport began to flourish, there were almost as many Mexican proprietors as Americans.

Steamboats bring cargo to Westport, another important departure point on the Missouri River.

Both Mexicans and Americans used Conestoga wagons. They were twelve or thirteen feet long. Their wooden bottoms sagged slightly. The boards at each end of the bed tipped gently outward. These features helped keep freight from shifting back and forth on rough roads.

Six or eight pliable wooden bows were arched over the high sides of the wagon beds. These bows were covered with one or, more often, two sheets of white osnaburg, a tough fabric resembling canvas. The wagon wheels were five feet tall, with iron rims about four inches wide. Wide iron tires didn't sink as deeply into soft ground as narrow ones did. A long train of Conestoga wagons was a marvelous sight—white tops, blue wagons, and red wheels, swaying along behind teams of horned oxen or long-eared mules.

Oxen were steady performers. Mules were more temperamental but bore up better on long trips where the ground was hard and grass thin. Mules were harnessed in pairs, generally four pairs to a wagon. They were controlled by a long jerk rein handled by an expert mule skinner who rode on the left mule of the pair closest to the wagons. Oxen were also worked in pairs. Each pair was joined by a heavy wooden yoke whose inverted U partly encircled each animal's neck. A bullwhacker wielding a huge whip walked beside the team, shouting commands. "Gee" meant turn right; "haw," left; "whoa!" stop. A heavily loaded wagon needed four yoke of oxen (eight animals, as with mules) to pull it along at an average rate of fifteen miles a day. At difficult places, such as the ford across the Arkansas River, teams would be doubled so that

Driving four yoke of oxen hitched to a big covered wagon was hard on both men and animals. Artist, Roy Anderson, Courtesy Pecos National Monument

sixteen straining animals could keep the wagon moving.

Because Indians were not a problem in eastern Kansas, the proprietors traveled singly or in small groups. They showed their importance by dressing well in broadcloth shirts and wide-brimmed hats. Some rode beside their wagons on sleek mules. Others sat in two-wheeled buggies covered with canvas against sun and rain. Their rendezvous with other proprietors was Council Grove, about 150

{ 24 }

miles west of Independence. Here a fine stand of hardwood trees arched over beautiful campgrounds covered with tall prairie grass. Unhappily, the grass at Council Grove and throughout eastern Kansas was alive with mosquitoes each spring. The zinging insects drove the animals and the people almost mad.

After the wagons had assembled at Council Grove, the proprietors elected an experienced frontiersman to be captain. His duties were to ride ahead of the caravan, picking out each day's resting place and each evening's campground. He selected and directed the advance crews that built roads across steep-banked ravines and laid mats of willow branches and grass across boggy places. The captain supposedly settled quarrels, maintained discipline, and assigned guards to patrol the camp throughout the night. Yet the very people who had elected him did not always obey him.

Big trains were divided into divisions of twenty-five or so wagons each. Lieutenants were elected to oversee each division's progress. The wagons of each division tried to travel close together. Mix-ups at creek crossings or the need of a wagon to stop for repairs sometimes prevented this.

The start of the assembled caravan from Council Grove was a scene of frantic confusion. In the dim light of dawn, bullwhackers scrambled to find and yoke their oxen and hitch them to the proper wagon. Proprietors and occasional sightseers rushed to saddle their horses or harness their buggies. As soon as each wagon was ready, its teamster bellowed, "All set!" After a number of those cries had sounded, the captain yelled, "Stretch out! Stretch out!" Whips cracked, drivers whooped, wheels rumbled, dogs barked, and the long procession took shape.

As the train moved deeper into Indian country and the land grew flatter, the wagons took to moving in two and often in four parallel columns. This gave a compactness to the moving train that discouraged attacks by the bold Kiowas and Comanches who lived south of the Arkansas River. Also a circle of wagons could be formed quickly if the vehicles traveled in parallel rows. Then each column could curve back on itself whenever the captain signaled for the train to prepare a circle around the campground.

Freight wagons traveling in four columns were difficult for Indians to attack. Also, the columns could move readily into a circle when the time came to camp.

It was important for the captain to search the land ahead of the train for campsites that provided plenty of grass, water, and fuel for cooking. Often the only fuel was lumpy disks of buffalo manure that contained enough grass to burn. Horses and mules were picketed outside the circle at the ends of long ropes. The oxen grazed loose, watched by night herders. Everyone in the train took a turn at standing watch. Mostly the guards had little to do other than look at the brilliant prairie stars and listen to the chewing of the animals and the howls of the coyotes.

On winter nights coyotes ventured close to the wagon camps, announcing their presence with eerie howlings.

A rest stop for teamsters and oxen.

The distance from Independence to Santa Fe over the Cimarron Branch was 775 miles. The trip took from seven to ten weeks. It could be tedious. On hot, dusty days the men yearned for rain to cool the sultry air. But they did not want so much rain that it produced thick mud that mired the wagons so completely in bad places that they would have to be unloaded before they could be pulled out of the bog.

The men ate only two meals a day. Breakfast came after

they had traveled three or four hours. Then they stopped to let the animals rest and graze. The food for the men was monotonous—bread baked in a Dutch oven, salt pork, and molasses, with occasional helpings of beans. A dinner of the same food came at dusk, after the circle had been completed and the animals cared for.

Furious lightning storms and a rare stampede of the animals stirred things up now and then. But the greatest excitement came when the first buffalo were sighted. Every man had brought along a rifle and ammunition. Off they charged toward the herd, the proprietors on horseback, the workers on foot. Often several buffalo were killed before the herd took alarm and ran off. The carcasses were butchered. The tastiest parts were taken to the wagons, to be roasted in front of the campfires. Uncooked pieces were sliced into thin strips. These were hung on cords or willow wands attached to the side of one or more wagons. There the meat dried into jerky under the hot sun of the plains. Huge swarms of flies formed buzzing clouds above each wagon that carried partly dried jerky.

A man who took sick or had an accident sometimes suffered cruelly. During his first trip with a caravan, sixteen-year-old Kit Carson helped amputate the infected arm of a teamster. The "doctors" had no anesthetic. The only tools were a knife and saw, and a heated bolt to sear the exposed veins and arteries so they would stop bleeding. The patient survived!

Early blizzards sometimes caught late caravans. When that happened some men and animals might freeze to death. During the early days of the trade, Indians killed a

As commerce grew more and more important, teamsters kept their wagons moving in every kind of weather.

few men who, through their own carelessness, invited trouble. The main goal of the Indians was the caravans' horses and the fine big mules the Americans had traded for in Santa Fe. In 1828 Comanches ran off a thousand head that were being driven to Missouri.

As the caravan toiled through the canyons that opened a way through the Sangre de Cristo Mountains, the wagons once more moved in single file. They passed the ghostly ruins of an abandoned Indian pueblo. The nights were cold, for the elevation was high, but the weary men relished seeing pine trees and smelling their fragrance

{ 30 }

again. At their last camp before rolling into Santa Fe, they washed, shaved, and put on the clean clothes they had kept in the kitchen wagons. The trip had succeeded; they wanted to strut!

Teamsters and bullwhackers, considerably cleaned up, celebrate their arrival in Santa Fe at a dance hall.

Stagecoach drivers were great show-offs as they dashed into Santa Fe.

The *pobladores* (townspeople) were as excited as the Americans. As the wagons creaked through the street to the plaza, the people thronged about. What wonderful things had the newcomers brought this time?

For many of the traders this was not the end of the trail. Some continued north to Taos or even as far south as Chihuahua. If goods did not sell quickly in Santa Fe, a proprietor might rent a store and spend the winter behind the counter before hurrying home in the spring to put together another venture. The fastest of the travelers was a daring native of Canada named Francis Xavier Aubry. Other merchants made only one round trip a year. On various occasions, Aubry made two. Once he rode alone across the plains, was captured and held briefly by Indians, and still reached Independence in record time!

The American merchants and their customers in New Mexico got along together because both sides benefited from their bargaining. Their governments, however, were not friendly. The immediate cause of the trouble was Texas. Until 1836 Texas had been a province of Mexico. That year Americans who had immigrated into the region revolted against Mexico and declared Texas an independent nation. The Mexicans refused to recognize the new nation. When the United States ignored Mexican protests and annexed Texas, war was inevitable. Shooting began in May 1846.

A deeper reason for the conflict was the determination of the ambitious young United States to spread across the entire continent. The Americans called this policy Manifest Destiny. They would not allow deserts, mountains, Indians, Englishmen in the Pacific Northwest or Mexicans in the Southwest to stand in their way.

The important battles of the Mexican War would be fought in the northeastern part of that country. In addition, the American government sent out a small force called "The Army of the West." It was commanded by Colonel Stephen Watts Kearny, a soldier well experienced in frontier travel and fighting. During the war Kearny would be promoted to the rank of brigadier general.

Brigadier General Stephen Watts Kearny commanded the Army of the West during the War with Mexico. The army assembled at Bent's Fort before invading New Mexico.

The government's strategy was for Kearny's force to conquer New Mexico first. If that proved as easy as most traders predicted, Kearny would leave a small contingent in Santa Fe and march the rest of his men across the southwestern deserts to California, another Mexican province.

The program brought almost unimaginable pandemonium to Independence, Westport, and, especially, Fort Leavenworth. The fort, located a few miles upstream from Westport, was Kearny's base. There he hurriedly assembled a force of 1,700 men—infantry, cavalry, and artillery. Most of the men were volunteers from the surrounding area. They could shoot and ride, but were not well disciplined. The real core of the Army of the West was 300 heavily armed, mounted dragoons who had served under Kearny for several years.

While the recruits were assembling in confusion—the

force never did get together at one time in one place—
fleets of river steamboats were unloading huge piles of
equipment at the three principal docks. To move this ma-
terial, the army purchased, during the year 1846, 15,000
oxen, 4,000 mules, and 1,500 wagons. Private traders
added to the problems. They expected the war would cause
prices in New Mexico to go up like swirls of frightened
birds. Experienced proprietors bought more goods than
usual. Speculators told themselves they, too, could make
money out of the turmoil. Altogether, 414 privately owned
wagons took to the trail that summer. This was more than
twice the number of wagons that had gone to Santa Fe
during the busiest of the previous years.

Not enough experienced bullwhackers and mule skin-
ners could be found to handle so many freight wagons
belonging both to the army and to individuals. As a result
many inexperienced men were hired. Inevitably they
wrecked a lot of wagons and left the corpses of many
starved or injured animals lying beside the trail.

The shambles made Kearny fear that the difficulties of
the dry crossing from the Arkansas River to the Cimarron
would be more than the army could handle. Accordingly
he ordered the troops and their supply wagons to continue
on up the Arkansas to the place called Bent's Fort. He also
ordered the traders' wagons to come together at the same
point. Some of them were carrying guns and bullets, and
the colonel did not want the munitions to reach the enemy
in Santa Fe.

The soldiers did not march west as a unit. First they
were organized into squads or companies at Fort Leaven-

A soldier drew this picture of Bent's Fort. Artist, Lachlan MacLean,
Museum of New Mexico

worth, given a little training, and sent out in segments. A
few companies of infantry might head out first, followed
by a battery of artillery, and behind them a company of
dragoons. There never were enough wagons to provide
food and equipment when needed. Rations were short.
The marchers grew hungrier and hungrier.

Nevertheless, the troops forged steadily ahead. Sometimes they sang in unison. More often they complained
loudly and profanely. They dodged rattlesnakes and
choked on their own dust. They amused themselves by
shooting at whatever game they saw—prairie dogs, big
jack rabbits, antelope, coyotes, a buffalo maybe, even
hawks and vultures soaring overhead. They did not inflict
much damage on the targets, but the constant shooting
worried the officers. Often they urged the men not to waste
so much ammunition. They might need it when they met
the enemy. Although the infantry were the noisiest grous-

{ 36 }

ers, they were the best marchers. Several companies of them reached Bent's Fort ahead of the mounted dragoons.

The size and strength of Bent's Fort surprised the troops. It had been built of adobe bricks in 1833 by gangs of Mexican workers hired in Taos and brought to the Arkansas by the brothers Charles and William Bent and their partner, Ceran St. Vrain. The fort's function was to provide a place where the traders could exchange manufactured goods for buffalo robes (hides) brought in by Cheyenne and Arapaho Indians who hunted far and wide

Charles Bent, his younger brother William, and Ceran St. Vrain built Bent's Fort, a famous Indian trading post, beside the Arkansas River within sight of the Rocky Mountains in 1833–34. Charles also ran a store in Taos. He was appointed governor of New Mexico after the American conquest in 1847. Rebels assassinated him in 1847.

William Bent lived at and managed Bent's Fort.

on the High Plains. A solid row of shops and dwellings, some two stories high, surrounded the fort's square, roof-less plaza. Attached to the back side of the building was a large walled enclosure for holding livestock. But no single structure could hold the gathering army. The riverbanks and the meadows for miles around were turned white by the covers of the wagons and the tents of the soldiers. The livestock and their herders competed noisily for what grass there was.

The easiest way from Bent's Fort into New Mexico—but hard enough!—was to continue west up the Arkansas

Kit Carson worked at Bent's Fort for a time. This imaginary picture shows the famous scout setting out from the fort on, perhaps, a trapping adventure.
Artist, Don Spaulding.

River to the vicinity of modern Pueblo, Colorado, and then swing southwest across Sangre de Cristo Pass into the San Luis Valley. By marching south on the *west* side of the Sangre de Cristo Mountains, the army could easily reach Taos, where Bent, St. Vrain & Company owned a store. From Taos a fairly good road led to Santa Fe. Colonel Kearny did not want to go that way, however. Many sturdy Mexican farmers and their Indian friends lived in the region and might cause trouble for the invading troops. So Kearny decided to cross Raton Pass instead and travel south on the *east* side of the Sangre de Cristo range. The land through which the army and the merchants would travel was dry and desolate. Not even Indians lived there regularly.

A trail but no road crossed Raton Pass. The travelers would have to build a way as they went. On hearing this, the teamsters who had been hired to manage the military wagons insisted that their contracts did not require them to do that kind of labor. Kearny thereupon ordered soldiers to do the work. Grumbling, the merchants decided to go along.

It was a dreadful ordeal. The men wrestled huge boulders out of the way, chopped trees, dug roadways in rocky ground. The hillsides were steep, the heat suffocating; alkali dust stung their eyes and throats. When oxen couldn't move a wagon, soldiers came to the rescue, a dozen men hauling on long ropes attached to the vehicle. Several wagons overturned, breaking their axles, injuring their teams, and scattering goods down the hillsides. One group of wagons spent a whole day traveling less than half a mile.

Next came the high volcanic plain east of the Sangre de Cristo Mountains. By then food was shorter than ever. The water in the creeks was bitter and generally fouled by livestock before the men could get at it. Balancing the discomforts was one tremendous bit of luck. After uttering angry threats and calling for thousands of volunteers to fight the invasion, Manuel Armijo, the governor of New Mexico, decided not to risk a battle. He was painfully short of trained soldiers and of guns and ammunition. So he fled, and on August 18, 1846, Kearny, by now a brigadier general, entered Santa Fe without firing a shot.

American dragoons enter Santa Fe during the War with Mexico. Artist, Don Spaulding

One of the first things he did was to rush messages to the troops still toiling up the Arkansas. Don't risk Raton! Use the dry crossing of the Cimarron! Later contingents of soldiers followed the advice. They suffered from thirst but arrived in Santa Fe in better shape than most of their predecessors.

After forming a territorial government for New Mexico, with Charles Bent as governor, Kearny marched on to California. Another column of Americans went south into Mexico to join the fighting there. Seeing how lightly the new territory was guarded, a group of Mexican and Pueblo Indians revolted in Taos. They killed Charles Bent and several other Americans, but the ill-planned rebellion was quickly crushed by troops storming north from Santa Fe under the leadership, in part, of Ceran St. Vrain. Later, in February 1848, representatives of defeated Mexico signed a peace treaty. Among other things, the treaty ceded the entire Southwest to the United States. From that point on, the Santa Fe Trail became wholly an American thorough-fare—and an American problem.

Before leaving New Mexico, General Kearny made a reckless promise. He told the people of New Mexico that the United States Army would protect them from the "wild" Indians of the Southwest.

By "wild," Kearny meant tribes of horse people who hunted game for food and lived in movable tents called tipis. By contrast, the Pueblo Indians of New Mexico were considered "tame." They lived in permanent towns, grew

This is how the Palace of the Governors looked shortly after the American occupation of New Mexico.

Supplying soldiers stationed in the Southwest after the war turned freighting into a big business. Francis X. Aubry, who once brought in three caravans in a single year, was one of the pioneers responsible for speeding up the commerce. Photographer, W. H. Brown, Center for Southwest Studies, University of New Mexico

crops, and sometimes helped the Hispanic (Spanish-speaking) New Mexicans in their struggles against the "wild" Indians.

The best known of the "wild" tribes of the Southwest were Apaches, Navajos, Utes, Comanches, and Kiowas. Altogether they numbered somewhere between 40,000 and 50,000 men, women, and children. For centuries they

{ 42 }

had stolen whatever they wanted from the New Mexicans. They were not going to let the United States change them. *They* had not been defeated by the whites. *They* had not signed any treaty of peace.

As part of its effort to keep General Kearny's promise, the United States built several forts and outposts in the territory. The soldiers who manned the fortifications had better weapons than the Indians, but they were not as good riders. As fighting increased, the number of troops in the territory rose from 1,000 men in 1848 to 3,500 in 1861. This was not a large number, but it was more than could be cared for by the poor residents of New Mexico. The people there raised barely enough food for themselves. Their clothing was homemade, with little to spare. Almost nothing was manufactured. Whatever the soldiers needed would have to be brought in from the outside, over the Santa Fe Trail.

The obstacles were enormous. One was winter weather. One officer told of a group "looking more like icicles of the North Pole than human beings." Fierce blizzards sometimes left campgrounds littered with the bodies of oxen that had frozen to death. Travelers passing such places occasionally amused themselves by arranging the bones in weird geometric patterns.

More deadly than the blizzards were Indian attacks. Major William Gilpin, who had reached Santa Fe shortly after Kearny, reported that during the first half of 1847, Indian raiders along the trail killed 47 Americans, seized 330 wagons, and drove off 6,500 head of livestock.

The Indians enjoyed the warfare. The columns of

clumsy wagons carried the kind of booty they relished. They learned how to pick out trains that were being handled by inexperienced and timid teamsters. Best of all, victory in combat brought fame to young warriors.

The Indians felt they were fighting to save their homelands from trespassers. The invaders cut down the small groves of cottonwood trees beside the streams where the Indians loved to camp. The work animals of the Americans stripped the grass from the Indians' favorite meadows. The thoughtless newcomers killed or frightened away the antelope and buffalo the tribes needed for food.

The whites tried different ways of meeting the problem. One was to show how much strength the Americans could muster. In the early spring of 1848, Major Gilpin swept down the Cimarron Branch as far as the Arkansas River with several companies of soldiers. They fought nine battles and killed 253 Indians. The tribes simply changed tactics. They slipped out onto the desolate plains of north-

Santa Fe in the 1850s. The center of the town has become crowded, but most inhabitants still live in small <u>ranchos</u> scattered around the outskirts.

eastern New Mexico looking for parties small enough for them to handle.

Two happenings illustrate the strategy. In October of 1849, an army surgeon named J. M. White was traveling in a carriage to a new post in New Mexico. With him were his wife, his small daughter, and their slave, a black woman. At first the Whites jogged along with a caravan commanded by Francis X. Aubry. After they were well inside New Mexico and were tired of dust and alkali water and boring travel, they decided to hurry ahead to Santa Fe. They had seen no Indians and felt they were close enough to the settlements to be safe. A couple of trader wagons went with them. Apaches caught them in one of their camps and killed every man. The Apaches held Mrs. White, the girl, and the black slave captive for a while and then killed them, too. As far as we know, these were the first females harmed on the Santa Fe Trail. For the trail was a commercial thoroughfare. Except for the families of army officers and traders, few women traveled it.

Another first occurred at Wagon Mound. Wagon Mound was a long ridge whose bulky shape reminded teamsters of a big wagon pulled by several yokes of oxen. A spring of good water in a cove at the base of the mound made it a good camping place. In May 1850, seven months after the White disaster, several teamsters accompanied a mail wagon running from Santa Fe to Fort Leavenworth. Apaches struck out of the night and killed the ten men. Government mail was scattered far and wide. This was the first attack on a mail wagon.

Passenger service began in 1851. A vehicle left either Independence or Santa Fe once a month. At first the stage-

Wagon Mound, rising starkly out of the High Plains of northeastern New Mexico, was named for its fancied resemblance to a freight wagon being pulled by oxen. Fort Union (not pictured) was located a few miles away, near the point where the Cimarron Branch and the Mountain Branch of the Santa Fe Trail came together. (See map.) Photographer, Three Hawks, Museum of New Mexico

coaches consisted of three wagons—one for passengers, one for mail, one for provisions. Often a fourth wagon filled with soldiers accompanied the procession along the dangerous stretch of trail between the crossing of the Arkansas River and Wagon Mound.

Completing the full 775-mile trip by stagecoach took from twenty-five to thirty days. A ticket cost $150. The passengers ate and slept on the ground with the soldiers and drivers. As the years passed, Concord coaches began to run as often as once a week. Wayside stations were built at intervals. They provided hard beds and poor meals for passengers, and fresh teams for the coaches. The trip nevertheless remained a miserable experience.

Stagecoaches began carrying regularly scheduled passengers from Missouri to New Mexico in the late 1850s. The journey was long, crowded, and uncomfortable. Passengers generally ate and slept on the ground with the drivers. Photographer, W. A. White, Museum of New Mexico.

Occasionally stagecoaches did have to outrun Indians. Mostly, though, escorts of soldiers discouraged Indian attacks.

Wagons trundle along San Francisco Street in Santa Fe.

The most important military post on the trail was Fort Union. It was located a few miles north of the point where the Mountain Branch of the trail from Raton Pass joined the Cimarron Branch. Like most of the military posts in the West, Fort Union was a collection of two-story buildings that served as dormitories, workshops, and offices. There was no wall around the installation. Indians were not likely to attack a post guarded by sentries and filled with troops.

{ 48 }

Fort Union served as a huge depot. Wagons from the East were unloaded there. The freight was then repacked for distribution to forts and outposts scattered throughout New Mexico and Arizona—sixteen of them at one period. The garrison at Fort Union also provided escorts for stagecoaches and small wagon trains. Big trains were expected to take care of themselves.

Big trains were common after the war with Mexico. Merchants (once called proprietors) no longer accompanied their wagons to Santa Fe. Instead they hired professional freighters. The military turned its huge business over to the firm of Russell, Majors, and Waddell. Each year after 1855, Russell, Majors, and Waddell put more

The wagon repair shop was the busiest part of Fort Union, the most important fort on the trail.

than five hundred high-sided Conestoga wagons on the trail to Fort Union. Trains were divided into units of twenty-five wagons each. Each was commanded by an expert wagon master. He allowed no nonsense from his tough bullwhackers, who were paid one dollar a day for their work.

The Civil War that broke out in the East between the Northern and Southern states in 1861 quickly spread to the Santa Fe Trail. The Confederate government dreamed

This is the first known photograph (1861) of wagons in the Santa Fe plaza. Trees that were planted before the war have grown to a respectable height.

of expanding across New Mexico and Arizona to the Pacific Ocean. The South would then have harbors on two oceans. It would also control the southern part of California, a new state rich from the great gold discoveries of 1848 and 1849. The North, of course, wanted to prevent the South's expansion.

During the winter of 1861–62, the South sent an army of Texans to the Rio Grande. Confusion filled the forts of New Mexico and Arizona. Soldiers who favored the South joined the invaders. Soldiers loyal to the North withdrew up the Rio Grande and across Glorieta Pass to Fort Union. There the officers set about creating a new army. With this force they hoped to protect the Santa Fe Trail and the new goldfields of Colorado. If reinforcements arrived soon enough from Colorado, the Northern soldiers might even be able to drive the Texans back out of New Mexico.

The Texans proved to be fine fighters. Sweeping up the Rio Grande Valley, they captured Albuquerque and Santa Fe. About March 20, a strong part of the force started toward Fort Union and Colorado. Eighty big wagons carried their supplies.

Unknown to the Confederates, several hundred Colorado volunteers had just reached Fort Union. On March 22, the best of these men, along with regular soldiers at Fort Union, started south on the trail to see what damage they could do to the Confederates. Their advance units collided in the narrow canyon leading into Glorieta Pass. This was March 26. Patches of snow still lay under the pine trees and on the north-facing slopes.

A small, fierce battle fought on the west side of the pass

Confederate soldiers, hoping to capture Fort Union during the Civil War, were stopped by Northern forces in battle at Glorieta Pass, in the Sangre de Cristo Mountains near Santa Fe.
Artist, Roy Anderson

settled nothing. Both sides withdrew to rest and care for their wounded. The camping grounds chosen by the Northern force were the meadows around a ramshackle stage station called Pigeon's Ranch. The Confederates camped at Johnson's Ranch on the west side of the pass. From there the Southern commander rushed messages to the main army at Santa Fe, asking for help.

The reinforcements arrived on March 27. The next day the Confederates crossed the pass and caught the Union troops by surprise. Rifle fire chattered, artillery boomed, bugles blared, cavalry charged. In an attempt to get behind the enemy, a detachment of Northerners climbed quietly onto a mesa south of the pass. They struggled westward through snow and forests. On reaching the rim of the canyon they saw, below them, the lightly guarded supply wagons of the enemy.

Yelling like fiends, the Northern troops plunged down the canyon slope. They overwhelmed the Confederate guard, set fire to the wagons, and slaughtered every horse, mule, and ox. A bloody business. But without food, ammunition, and blankets, the Confederates had to retreat. New Mexico and probably the entire Southwest were saved for the North.

The war changed travel routes. Until then most caravans left the Arkansas River a little west of today's Dodge City, Kansas, and rolled southwest along the Cimarron Branch. This road was shorter than the route up the Arkansas past Bent's Fort and over Raton Pass. But when war broke out, Union officers began worrying that Southern raiders might block the eastern end of the trail. Worse, the war between the whites excited the Comanche and Kiowa Indians. They realized many soldiers were being moved east to fight there, and they began roaming the Branch for plunder. The army accordingly ordered its supply trains to follow the longer Mountain Branch to Fort Union. Most commercial trains turned to the same mountainous route.

The change of routes did not end the Indian problem. Civilians traveling up the Arkansas River toward the Colorado goldfields continually disturbed the Indians lands. If the Indians objected, volunteers from Colorado rode out to help the newcomers. The fighting grew deadly. One bitterly cold night late in November of 1864, volunteer troops massacred more than two hundred peaceful Cheyenne and Arapaho Indians in their camp at Sand Creek, several miles north of the trail in eastern Colorado.

That same month, November 1864, troops commanded by Kit Carson fought a desperate battle with Comanches and Kiowas at Adobe Walls in the Texas Panhandle. Carson had intended to punish the natives for their raids in New Mexico and along the Santa Fe Trail. As matters turned out, the Americans were barely able to escape.

Conflicts continued into the 1870s, but time was running out for the Indians. The coming of railroads onto the plains completed their defeat. In the Southwest the principal railroad was the Atchison, Topeka, and Santa Fe, commonly shortened to Santa Fe. During the 1870s its tracks moved slowly westward up the Arkansas River. Wagons met the trains at each new railhead—that is, at the farthest point the tracks had reached. Column after column of ox-drawn vehicles carried the freight they picked up over Raton Pass to Fort Union. Piles of supplies for fighting the Indians grew bigger and bigger. Moreover, the steam trains could carry troops as quickly as they could carry merchandise. Faced with a power they could not overcome, the Indians agreed to settle on reservations.

By this time, Raton Pass was fairly easy to cross, thanks to Richens Lacy Wootton. Tall, muscular, and soft-spoken, Wootton was commonly known as Uncle Dick. A friend of Kit Carson, he had roamed the West since 1836 as a trapper, Indian trader, army scout, wagon freighter, and storekeeper in the infant town of Denver, Colorado.

When traffic on the Mountain Branch increased, Uncle Dick settled on a farm near the base of Raton Pass. Hiring crews of Mexicans, he built a road twenty-seven miles long over the pass from southern Colorado into northern New Mexico. The legislatures of both territories granted him a charter that allowed him to collect tolls from everyone who used his road. He also built a hotel for teamsters and stagecoach passengers near the Colorado side of the trail.

Richens Lacy Wootton (Uncle Dick), trapper, scout, and friend of Kit Carson, built a toll road for wagons across Raton Pass between Colorado and New Mexico. Later he sold the right-of-way to the Atchison, Topeka, and Santa Fe Railroad—the Santa Fe for short.

In 1878, the Santa Fe Railroad reached the northern foot of the pass. The company bought Uncle Dick's wagon road for a fine sum. The next problem was to bore a tunnel through the mountain two hundred feet below the pass. If tracks went through this tunnel, locomotives would not have to burn huge amounts of expensive coal to haul freight trains over the last high part of the route.

The time needed for building the tunnel could be cut in half if workers dug and blasted from both ends at the same time. In order to bring materials to workers on the south side of the mountain, the railroad company brought in trainloads of lightweight rails. Using these, they created a series of breathtaking zigzags over the top of the pass and

Indians watch a railroad train approach the Rocky Mountains. They must have sensed that speedy transportation of troops, along with the killing of the last buffalo, would change their lives forever.

Temporary rails let trains zigzag across the top of Raton Pass while a tunnel was being bored lower down.

Nearly sixty years passed between the arrival of the first American trader in Mexican Santa Fe and the appearance of the railroad. During that same time the Santa Fe plaza changed from a bleak, unadorned square to the cheerful gathering place pictured here. Artist, F. X. Grosshenny, Museum of New Mexico

into New Mexico. Thanks to the fast movement of supplies to both sides of the mountain, the Raton Tunnel was completed on July 7, 1879.

Special locomotives were needed to haul heavy freight through the rugged country. The first big steam engine to pull cars through the tunnel was named Uncle Dick. It was an appropriate name. Uncle Dick Wootton had first traveled west with a wagon train when he was twenty years old. Now, nearly half a century later, he had helped bring the first mountain locomotive to the Southwest. Those early engines look small to us today. But they could haul as much freight in a week as Russell, Majors, and Waddell's 3,500 oxen could haul in a year.

A locomotive tests Raton Tunnel. Photographer, J. R. Riddle, Museum of New Mexico

In 1880 steam locomotives seemed like giant miracles to the people of New Mexico. Photographer, Ben Wittick, Museum of New Mexico

The Santa Fe wagon trade passed into history.

Yet you can still see, near Fort Union, miles and miles of ruts in the dry ground under the thin grass. They are the marks of a nation that called on some of its strongest men to help it extend ever westward, no matter what stood in the way.

A Comanche warrior who once fought American troops poses for a picture in 1886. Photographer, J. R. Riddle, Museum of New Mexico

Its usefulness ended, Fort Union collapsed into ruins. Today those stark remnants are a National Monument. Photographer, Alice Bullock, Museum of New Mexico

These wagon ruts, worn over the years deep into the sod of the plains near Fort Union, remain as enduring mementos of America's westward expansion. Photographer, Harold Walter, Museum of New Mexico

INDEX

Page numbers in italics refer to photos.

To Brendan, Siobhan, and Merritt

Map on pages 4 and 5 by Leonard Everett Fisher.

Acknowledgments for some illustrations appear at the end of their captions. For all others, grateful acknowledgment is made to the following organizations:

Center for Southwest Studies, University of New Mexico, pages 13, 17, 18, 37, 42; Huntington Library, pages 10, 14, 16, 20, 22, 26, 27, 28, 30, 31, 32, 44, 47, 56; Kansas State Historical Society, page 21; Museum of New Mexico, pages 48, 49, 50, 57; Western History Department, Denver Public Library, pages 34, 37, 55.

Library of Congress Cataloging-in-Publication Data
Lavender, David Sievert, 1910–
The Santa Fe Trail / David Lavender. — 1st ed.
p.   cm.
Includes index.
ISBN 0-8234-1153-2
1. Santa Fe Trail—Juvenile literature.   I. Title.
F786.L382   1995   94-16638   CIP   AC
978—dc20